FOR MY FATHER.

First published in the United States of America
in 2018 by Chronicle Books LLC.

Originally published in Portugal in 2017 under the title
A Cidade dos Animais by Orfeu Negro, www.orfeunegro.org.

Copyright © 2017 by Joan Negrescolor.
English translation copyright © 2018 by Chronicle Books LLC.

Library of Congress Cataloging-in-Publication Data available.

ISBN 978-1-4521- 7029-9

Manufactured in China.

Original Orfeu Negro design by Rui Silva.
Original text edited by Carla Oliveira.
Case design by Alice Seiler.
The illustrations in this book were rendered digitally.

10 9 8 7 6 5 4 3 2 1

Chronicle Books LLC
680 Second Street
San Francisco, California 94107

Chronicle Books—we see things differently.
Become part of our community at www.chroniclekids.com.

ANIMAL CITY

JOAN NEGRESCOLOR

chronicle books · san francisco

SHE KNOWS ALL THE
PATHS AND SMELLS THERE.

THIS IS HER SECRET PLACE.
THIS IS WHERE THE ANIMALS AND PLANTS LIVE . . .

AND WHERE LOST OBJECTS ARE FOUND.

NINA LIKES TO WATCH
THE FLURRY OF THE CITY.

HER FRIENDS ARE
ALWAYS SO HAPPY
TO SEE HER!

NINA BRINGS STORIES TO
READ TO THE ANIMALS.

THE MONKEYS LIKE STORIES
ABOUT OTHER WORLDS:
JOURNEYS TO THE MOON,
ESCAPADES IN OUTER SPACE,
AND ALIEN ADVENTURES.

THE FLAMINGOS LIKE MYTHS AND
LEGENDS ABOUT GODS, DRAGONS,
AND BEASTS WITH SEVEN HEADS.

AND THE SNAKE PREFERS POEMS ABOUT
THE SEA, SAILORS, AND STORMS.

BUT THE STORY
THE ANIMALS
LIKE BEST . . .

THE STORY TAKES PLACE IN A QUIET SPOT . . .

AND WHERE NATURE NOW RUNS WILD.

NINA CALLS IT "ANIMAL CITY."
SOON SHE WILL BE BACK FOR A NEW STORY.